RUSS THOMPSON

STANDING FOR ME

Finding Forward
Books

Published by Finding Forward Books.
P.O. Box 8182, Long Beach, California 90808.
www.findingforwardbooks.com

Editing by Laura Perkins. Series concept by Pam Sheppard. Text set in Open Dyslexic Mono. Cover photo by Shutterstock.

Library of Congress Control Number 2025916974
ISBN 979-8-265817-36-5 (Amazon paperback)
ISBN 978-1-964809-04-5 (Ingram paperback)
FILE FF013-29B-20251208

Summary: An adult who struggles with reading strives to succeed in college.

BISAC Subject Codes: | YOUNG ADULT FICTION / Emotions and Feelings | YOUNG ADULT FICTION / Self-Esteem and Self Reliance | YOUNG ADULT FICTION /School and Education / General

Lexile Measure HL560L

For Betty Jean,
our kids,
and grandkids.

CONTENTS

1 NEVER

AFTERNOON. Food Giant Market. I push my shopping cart around the corner to the potato chips.

My jeans are dirty. My work boots are scuffed and worn. My orange work shirt from Price Mart has grease on it.

There she is, Ms. Gulliver.

I haven't seen her for two years.

She was my favorite teacher at Edison High School.

But I don't want her to see me in my work clothes.

I turn and go to the dairy
section.

But she comes around the
corner.

"Clark, is that you?" she
asks. "How are you doing?"

I try to smile back. I want
her to think I'm successful.

"Everything is great," I say.
"I'm getting good grades at
Jasper. My next stop will be
Raymond State."

"I'm so happy to hear that,"
she says. "I know you will go
far."

She glances into my cart.

I have canned chili, macaroni
and cheese, cookies, and hot
dogs.

I wish I had something
healthy. I feel better when she

smiles.

"Be sure to come back to Edison for College Day," she says. "It's in April. It would be wonderful for the students to hear how you're doing at Jasper."

It's great to see her.

But I feel bad about what I said.

I never even applied to Jasper Community College.

2 CHANCE TO MAKE

I GET TO OUR HOUSE, park on the street, and walk up the driveway to my place.

It's an extra room that Dad and I added on to the back of the garage. It has a bed, a bathroom, and a little kitchen.

There's not much space to walk around.

But it's mine. I pay rent on it.

I get out my cooking pot, dump in a can of chili, add some rice, and put it on my mini-stove.

I also put a bag of vegetables into the microwave.

The nice thing about chili and rice is that it's easy to make.

Also, there's only one pot to clean.

My phone beeps. It's a text from Katie. She wants to know about tomorrow night.

I text back that I'll pick her up at six.

Work was good today. I'm the best order-puller at the warehouse.

I might be getting a raise.

I also have a chance to make supervisor someday.

3 WILL NOT

WAREHOUSE. I clock in and go to the staging area by the loading docks.

It's a huge building, about fifteen acres. We send stuff to thirty-six different Price Mart stores.

I bump fists with Eugene and Willis.

"Clark, anything new?" Eugene asks.

"All good," I say.

"Me too" says Willis.

Our supervisor, Tommy, comes out

for his morning talk. He's a big guy with strong arms and a thick neck.

There are eighteen of us. We form a semi-circle facing him.

"Any announcements?" Tommy asks.

Willis raises his hand. "My wife and I are having a party for our daughter's first birthday this Saturday. If any of you want to come, let me know. There will be food and everything."

We clap and holler for Willis.

Maybe Katie will come with me.

Nobody has anything else to say. Tommy starts his daily pep talk.

"The first thing I want to remind you about is safety," he says. "Keep your eyes open, think, and be careful. There was an accident at the Munson warehouse yesterday. Two forklifts hit, and a guy had his arm crushed."

I look at my arm. I hope it never happens to me.

"And remember what I said about Price Mart's new program to pay for college expenses," Tommy says. "Business administration is a great way to go if you want to advance within the company."

He looks straight at me.

Tommy has been bugging me about enrolling at Jasper College for the last month.

But I hate school.

And I like what I'm doing in the warehouse.

I will not be going to Jasper College.

4 REAL FUTURE

I GO TO MY PALLET RIDER. It's the kind where you stand at the front and it pulls two pallets behind you.

I turn on the console and put on the headset. The electronic voice tells me to do the safety check.

I listen to what it says, check my pallet rider, and say done after each step.

I don't have to read or anything. ALL I have to do is work.

The voice on the headset says, "Row Q, spot 429." I go forward.

When I get to the spot, the voice says, "Item AB-7892, Ruffy Dog Food, three cases."

I load the boxes onto the pallet and say, "Item AB-7892, three cases, done."

The voice says, "Row C, spot 389."

I go off to get more boxes. Thirty minutes later, I'm finished.

I go to the staging area and wrap the pallets in plastic.

Tommy comes over with his handheld and checks everything. "Clark," he says. "Looks good."

I think about Dad. He said he's proud of me.

I'm working, I make good money, and I get health benefits. I have a solid job with a real future.

5 DOESN'T SAY

FRIDAY EVENING. I pull to the curb in front of Katie's house.

Usually, she watches for me and comes right out.

But not tonight.

I turn off the engine and walk to the front door.

I'm glad when she answers.

But something is wrong.

She doesn't smile like she usually does.

And she doesn't hold my hand when we walk to my truck.

I start the engine and pull away from the curb.

I wish she would talk.

But she doesn't say anything.

6 THEY DON'T

CONROY MALL. Katie and I go up the escalator to the food court.

She holds my hand. But I don't think she wants to.

We order burgers and sit in the back. Everything feels wrong tonight.

"Katie, how were your classes today?" I ask.

She usually smiles. But her face is blank. "I got an A on my political science paper," she says. "I also met with my advisor.

Everything is ready for me to transfer from Jasper to Munson State next fall."

I smile when I look back at her.

But that's not how I feel.

Munson State is seventy-five miles away. If she goes there, I'll never see her.

"Have you thought any more about Raymond State?" I ask.

"I know it's close," she says. "But my mom and dad both went to Munson. They said it was good for them to get away from home."

She looks away. I feel like I'm losing her.

She might as well say it would be good for her to get away from me.

The buzzer they gave me for our food goes off.

It gives me an excuse to get up.

    Maybe this isn't happening.

    Maybe it will be okay.

    But when I get back, Katie still
has that blank look on her face.

    We begin eating.

    Burgers and fries are my
favorite.

    But they don't taste like
anything tonight.

7 OVER

WE FINISH EATING and go to a movie like we always do.

It's a comedy.

And she laughs.

But when I reach over to hold her hand, it's not there.

When the movie ends, she walks out with her arms folded in front of her.

It's over.

8 WISH I KNEW

SATURDAY AFTERNOON. I leave my room and walk past the side door of the garage.

The weights are clanging. Dad is lifting weights inside.

I step through the door and stand behind the bench to spot him as he does bench presses.

His face turns red. The muscles in his arms strain.

But he finishes ten reps.

"Clark, let's add more," he says.

We put five more pounds on each

end. The total now is 200 pounds.

He pushes up the bar and does six reps.

"Not bad," I say. "But are you ready to get beat?"

"Not today," he says.

I take off my jacket. "We'll see."

We change the weight to 180. I lie on the bench and push it up ten times.

It's easy.

Next, we put on 190 pounds. I do it eight times.

It's harder. But I know I can do more.

I stand up to stretch and swing my shoulders.

"Dad, put it at 200," I say. "I'm feeling good."

I do it six times.

We're tied.

"Let's go to 205," Dad says. "Whoever does the most reps wins."

We add the weight. Dad goes first. He pushes it up three times.

Now, it's my turn.

I push it up four times.

Dad rings the victory bell and shakes my hand.

He smiles. But I see sadness in his eyes.

"Dad, is something wrong?" I ask.

"It's okay," he says. "Everything is fine."

That's what he says. But something is bothering him.

"I thought I had a new job lined up," he says. "But it fell through yesterday."

I see the pain in his eyes.

"The warehouses are getting more

automated, and there are fewer jobs," he says. "But don't worry. Something will come up."

It's been two months since he lost his warehouse job at Cost Rite.

I can tell it's tearing him up inside.

I wish I knew what to say.

9 HAPPENED TO ME

DINNER. Kitchen. Dad and I sit down. Mom brings spaghetti to the table.

"Clark, how was your week?" Mom asks.

"It was fine," I say. "But my boss wants me to go back to school."

"What do you mean?" Dad asks.

"Price Mart has a program that pays for college. They want people to go into business administration. But I like what I'm doing in the warehouse."

"The warehouse may be good for

now," Dad says. "But what about your future?"

"What do you mean?" I ask.

"Think about it," he says. "Look what happened to me."

10 CHANGE HER MIND

LATER. Dinner is over. I go back to my place.

Things are looking up.

With my next raise coming, it won't be long before I can get a new truck.

It won't be brand new. But it will have a good motor, no dents or scratches, and a sound system.

I think about Katie.

Maybe she will change her mind about me when she sees it.

11 MY JOB

MONDAY MORNING. Warehouse. I'm always glad when I get here.

Then I think about Dad.

I know he wants to work. It's tearing him apart to stay at home.

I clock in, go to the staging area, and bump fists with Willis and Eugene.

Tommy comes out for his morning pep talk.

But something is wrong. He doesn't smile like he usually does.

"I need to let you know about the

company," he says. "Profits have been going down for the last few months. I was told this morning that there might be layoffs. Julie from the union will be here at lunch to talk to you."

This is a shock. I can't believe what he's saying.

I look at the others. They all seem worried.

"Go ahead and get started," Tommy says. "And remember. Be careful and be safe."

I walk slowly to my pallet rider, turn on the console, and put on my headset.

Tommy said to be careful.

But what if I lose my job?

12 NOT ANYMORE

LUNCH. Break room. I sit across the table from Willis and Eugene.

Julie, from the union, comes in. She's old, probably in her fifties. She walks with a limp and wears her red union shirt.

"Everybody is hoping there won't be a layoff," she says. "But you have to be ready. The union will help you apply for unemployment benefits. But you need to think ahead."

Pete raises his hand. "How much

will we get if we have to go on unemployment?"

"The maximum is $450 a week," she says. "That's why you have to think ahead."

Willis raises his hand. "Tommy said last week that the company has a program to pay for college costs. Will that still happen if there's a layoff?"

"If you get laid off, it won't," she says. "It will only be available to those who are working."

It's silent when she leaves.

"If I get laid off, I don't have anything else I can do," Willis says.

"Same for me," Eugene says. "And I know they're not hiring at any of the other warehouses around here."

Everything was great when I came

to work this morning.

I thought I was going to be here forever.

Not anymore.

13 WORRY HER MORE

AFTER WORK. Burger House. I put in my order and find a seat in the back.

My phone buzzes. It's Mom.

"Clark, I'm calling because I need to talk to you about Dad without him listening," she says. "Things are getting harder for him. When he gets on the computer to apply for jobs, he just stares at the screen and does nothing. Then he goes out to the garage to lift weights. Or he does yardwork and fiddles around the house."

I don't know what to say. It feels like he's giving up.

"I heard there might be layoffs at Price Mart," she says. "Is that true?"

"Everything is fine," I say. "Nobody has talked about any problems."

I don't like lying.

But I don't want to worry her more.

14 DON'T WANT

EVENING. My place. I sit at the table and look at my phone.

I feel like calling Katie. Maybe there's still a chance we can get back together.

I make the call and wait for her to pick up.

But it goes to her voice mail.

I could leave a message.

But I don't.

I get on my laptop and look at the website for Jasper Community College.

The business administration program shows pictures of smiling people doing office jobs.

The jobs pay more than working in the warehouse.

But when I think of school, all the bad memories come back.

I just don't want to go.

15 OUT OF THE WAY

TUESDAY. After lunch. I go to my pallet rider and run through the safety check.

Everything is good.

The voice in the headset tells me to go to Row G. I push the controller and move forward.

I think about Dad. I know he wishes he was working.

I think about Katie. I hope we can get back together again.

I get to Row G and step off my pallet rider to grab a case of granola bars.

Eugene comes around the corner on his forklift.

He's going too fast.

He's coming right at me.

I can't get out of the way.

16 SORRY

I LIE ON MY BACK. I try not to scream.

My foot is burning with pain.

Eugene kneels next to me.

"Clark, hang on," he says. "The paramedics are on the way."

I look at my leg.

My pants are soaked in blood. My foot is pointing sideways.

Eugene squeezes my hand. "Clark, I'm so sorry," he says.

17 JUST THERE

HOSPITAL. I open my eyes. Mom and Dad look down at me.

Mom's eyes are red. She's been crying.

"Clark, can you hear me?" she asks.

"Where am I?"

"We're back in your hospital room," she says.

"Are they done?" I ask.

"It's all over," Dad says. "The surgery was a success."

"The doctor told us you broke

seven bones in your foot," Mom says.

I look at my legs.

My left foot is okay. I can move
my toes.

My right foot is wrapped with
bandages.

I thought it would hurt.

But I don't feel anything.

It's just there.

18 STOPPED NOW

LATER. I look out the window of my
hospital room. It's dark outside.

Mom and Dad sit next to me. Their
eyes are closed. Dad is snoring.

I remember how I felt when I
started working in the warehouse.

I was on my way.

Everything was great.

Nothing could stop me.

But I'm stopped now.

19 WORKING AGAIN

FOUR WEEKS LATER. Monday morning. I get on my crutches, lock the door, and walk down the driveway to the sidewalk.

The appointment for my foot is at ten-thirty.

Mom is at work. Dad has another warehouse job.

That means I'm on my own to get to the doctor's office.

I walk three blocks and reach the bus stop.

I think about Dad and his new

job.

The pay is less. But he's smiling again.

He took Mom and me to dinner at Golden Grill to celebrate.

He feels good about himself because he's working.

I think about my foot.

The pain is still bad.

But I'll be working again, too.

20 WHAT TO SAY

ANOTHER FOUR WEEKS LATER. Exam room.
Dr. Beckett walks in.

He usually smiles. But not today.
Something is wrong.

"Clark, how has your foot been
feeling?" he asks.

"I still have pain. I can't put
weight on it."

"I looked at your x-rays," he
says. "I have some concerns about
how the bones have been healing."

He shows me the x-rays on the
computer screen. I see the screws

holding the heelbone together. They look like they came from a hardware store.

"Your top ankle bone, the talus, still has cracks in it," Dr. Beckett says. "You also have cracks in your first and second metatarsals. Those are the bones in the middle of your foot that connect to your toes. That's why you're having pain when you put weight on your foot."

I look at the floor. I don't want him to see my face. I thought the bones would be healed by now.

"What happens next?" I ask.

"I want to keep the splint on and have you stay on the crutches for another four weeks," he says. "Ideally, the foot will show healing after that. If not, it may be necessary to consider another surgery."

Another surgery? He acts like
it's no big deal.

Everything is falling apart.

I don't know what to say.

21 HOPES UP

I LEAVE DR. BECKETT'S OFFICE on my crutches and get on the bus.

My foot hurts when I walk to my seat.

But it feels better when I sit down.

I get off the bus at Burger House.

The pain starts again.

I was stupid to get my hopes up.

22 WHEN SHE LEAVES

BURGER HOUSE. I order a cheeseburger
and find a seat by the window.

Everyone looks busy. They all
have places to go after they eat.

But not me.

The door opens.

Some girls come in. One of them
is Katie.

I watch them order.

Katie acts like she doesn't see
me. Then she walks over and sits
across from me.

"Clark, I heard about your

accident," she says. "Is it getting better?"

"I don't know. I go back to see the doctor in four weeks."

"What happens after that?" she asks.

"It's hard to say. It's taking a long time to heal."

She looks at me like she's waiting for me to say more.

I say nothing.

I'm glad when she leaves.

23 I WISH

MY PLACE. Late afternoon.

I turn on the TV, lean back on the recliner, and look at the ice bag on my foot.

Maybe in four weeks, I will be back to normal.

Or maybe I won't.

There's a knock on my door. It's Willis and Eugene.

We bump fists like we do in the warehouse. They come in and sit across from me.

"Clark, we have good news,"

Eugene says. "There's not going to be a layoff."

It's a relief to hear him say that. I'm glad that nobody will be losing their job.

"When are you coming back?" Willis asks me.

"I don't know," I say. "It's taking a long time to heal."

"I hope it's soon," Eugene says. "We're waiting for you."

I think about my days pulling orders.

I wish I could go back to the warehouse tomorrow.

24 OVER

FOUR WEEKS LATER. Dr. Beckett's office. It's been twelve weeks since the surgery.

"Clark, how's it been feeling?" he asks.

"It still hurts. I was hoping it would be better by now."

He takes off the splint and bandages. The scars are fully healed. All the bruising is gone.

He turns the computer screen toward me so I can see the new x-rays.

"I was concerned that you might
need another surgery," Dr. Beckett
says. "But the x-rays look good now.
Your foot just needs more time to
heal."

"How long before I can start
walking again?"

"It's hard to say," he says. "You
still have a long way to go. If you
try to rush it, you will damage your
foot more."

"What do I need to do?"

"Keep wearing the splint and stay
on your crutches," he says. "I'll
know more after I see you next
month."

"When do you think I'll be able
to go back to work?"

"I hate to say it," he says. "But
with the amount of damage you have,
even when the bones fully heal,

going back to work in the warehouse
would be out of the question. You
need to think seriously about
getting a job where you won't have
to be on your feet."

I smile and say thanks.

But that's not how I feel.

My warehouse days are over.

25 WORSE

AFTERNOON. My place. I think about what Dr. Beckett said.

I open my laptop and do a search for jobs that don't require standing.

Business administration is one of them. I think about the program at Jasper College.

Ms. Gulliver used to say that college was nothing more than grade thirteen.

She said that if you could make it in high school, you could make it in college.

But that's her. She was always saying stuff like that.

I think about how hard it was for me at Edison High School.

If I go to Jasper College, it's going to be worse.

26 MIDNIGHT

EVENING. I leave my place and go up the back steps to the kitchen.

Mom made soup and salad. Dad comes in. We all sit down together.

"Clark, what did the doctor say?" Mom asks.

"He said the bones need more time to heal. Also, I can't go back to work in the warehouse."

"Is that because of the walking?" Dad asks.

"And the standing," I say. "Even after it heals, he doesn't think my foot will be able to handle it."

"Have you thought any more about Jasper College?" Mom asks.

"They have a good business program," I say. "And Price Mart will still pay for it."

"That's great," Dad says. "You should go for it."

I take a bite of salad and look out the window.

It's easy for him to say that.

But the classes at Jasper are hard.

"When do you have to decide?" Mom asks.

"I have to decide this evening. The deadline to register for the spring quarter is midnight."

27 NEVER WENT

FIVE WEEKS LATER. Monday morning.
It's the first day of the spring
quarter.

I catch the bus for Jasper
College and climb in carrying my
crutches.

My foot still hurts to put weight
on it, so I have to be careful.

I find my way to a seat near the
middle. The bus pulls away.

I hate the idea of going back to
school.

It's going to be hard with all

the reading I will have to do.

I look down at the splint on my foot.

Dad says I'm doing the right thing by going to Jasper College.

But what about him?

If college is so great, how come he never went?

28 REQUIRED CLASS

JASPER COLLEGE. English 101. It's like a big theater with desks where you look down at the front.

I find an empty seat where I can stick my leg out.

The professor comes to the front. She's about fifty, with glasses and gray hair.

"I'm Dr. Maxwell," she says. "This is English 101. You will learn to read and understand complex materials in this class. You will also learn to analyze and write

about what you read. The skills you
learn here will help you in any
career where you have to understand
information and use it."

She stops and looks at each of
us. She's all business. I wonder
what she thinks when she looks at
me.

"You will sit in small groups to
discuss your reading assignments,"
she says. "You will also write
essays on paper during class to
discuss your opinions about what you
have read."

It scares me.

I won't be able to copy from the
internet.

But I don't have a choice.

This is a required class.

29 UNTIL I KNOW IT

EVENING. My place. I sit in the easy chair and prop up my foot.

The story I have to read is "The Lottery," by Shirley Jackson.

I begin reading. It's very hard.

I can read the words. But it's hard to understand.

I reach the end, go back to the first page, and begin reading again.

I'm going to keep reading it until I know it.

30 HAND SHAKES

WEDNESDAY MORNING. English 101. I almost trip on my crutches as I look for a place to sit.

Dr. Maxwell comes to the front.

"I hope you all did your reading," she says. "I started you off with 'The Lottery' to show you the power of a compelling story."

I feel like I'm ready. I didn't like the story at first. But I read it five times. Now, I understand it.

"I want you to get into groups of three to discuss the story," Dr.

Maxwell says. "You will get twelve minutes"

I end up in a group with Natalie and Vincent. They both seem very smart.

"I got fooled at the beginning," Natalie says. "I thought it was going to be a heartwarming story about people in a small town."

"Me too," Vincent says. "I was shocked at the end. I couldn't believe it when they started throwing rocks."

I have ideas I would like to talk about. But I freeze.

I don't want Natalie and Vincent to think I'm stupid.

They talk more about the story. They also give me chances to break in.

But I don't speak up. I don't

feel smart enough.

Dr. Maxwell comes to the front again.

"This next part is writing your in-class essays," she says. "I want you to explain an event in the story, your reaction, and why you feel that way."

I take out a piece of paper and try not to be nervous.

"Please begin," Dr. Maxwell says. "You will get twenty-five minutes."

I look at my paper.

I know what to write.

But my hand shakes.

31 ONE OF THEM

AFTER CLASS. I leave the English building and walk down the sidewalk on my crutches.

I finished my essay. I should be glad. But I know the spelling is terrible.

When Dr. Maxwell sees my paper, she's going to think it was written by a third grader.

There's a building off to the side with a sign that says College Skills Center.

I should go inside.

They can probably help me with my
reading and writing.

But there are a lot of former
students from Edison who go here.

What if one of them sees me?

32 SHOULD HAVE

MONDAY MORNING. I climb into the bus and find a seat. It's my second week at Jasper College.

I knew it was going to be hard.

And it is.

I was up again studying last night until after midnight.

I remember my time at Edison High School.

My reading wasn't good.

And I hated going to class.

But I knew how to fake it.

I would smile at the teachers and

sit up straight to act like I was
interested.

I would copy from the internet
instead of doing my homework the
right way.

And I could usually guess right
on the multiple-choice tests.

But you can't fake it in Dr.
Maxwell's class.

You have to know it.

I should have worked at Edison
instead of playing around.

33 BAD

ENGLISH 101. Dr. Maxwell hands back the essays we wrote last week.

Most of the people smile when they get their papers back.

But when I get mine, about half the words are underlined in red.

They're the ones I didn't know how to spell.

She put a note at the top. It says to see her in her office.

It's going to be bad.

34 REALLY TRYING

AFTER CLASS. I sit across from Dr. Maxwell in her office.

The room is cramped, with books and papers piled on the shelves.

I try not to be nervous. I'm surprised when she smiles.

"Clark, I was impressed when I read your essay," she says. "You knew the story well. You saw things that the other students didn't see."

I can't believe what she's telling me. I thought she was going to say my essay was terrible.

"How do you feel about your spelling?" she asks.

"I know it's bad. It's always been that way."

"What about your reading?" she asks.

"That's also been hard for me."

"Do you know about the College Skills Center?"

"I know where it is. But I've never been inside."

"I want you to go there today," she says. "If you do what they say and work hard, you can improve your spelling. You can also bring up your reading."

I never thought this would happen.

She's really trying to help me.

35 GOING TO TRY

LATER. I sit across from Harold, a tutor in the College Skills Center.

"Clark, we can do a lot to help you with your spelling," he says. "We can also help you with your reading. It will not be easy. But if you work hard every day, you will gradually improve."

I've heard this before. But it hasn't worked.

"I want you to start off by doing two things," he says. "First, I want you to read the front page of the newspaper every day. You can get a free subscription through the college that you can read on your laptop. Second, I want you to read in a book every day. Doing these things will improve your reading skills. You will also learn about what is happening in the world. And the more you read, the more your spelling will improve."

It sounds too good to be true.

But I'm going to try.

36 LIKE IT

AFTERNOON. Jasper College Library. I get on my laptop to look at the Conroy Courier.

There's a story about the mayor of Conroy and how he wants to reduce crime.

There's a story about Congress passing a bill to increase funding for schools.

I also read a story about a restaurant that caught on fire.

It's the first time I've ever read the newspaper.

I didn't know it could be so interesting.

Next, I open up the book I checked out, *A Wanted Man*, by Lee Child.

It's about a guy named Jack Reacher who is hitchhiking at night through Nebraska.

When he finally gets picked up, he doesn't know that the people in the car are wanted by the FBI.

I've never read a whole book before.

I think I'm going to like it.

37 WHATEVER IT TAKES

MY PLACE. I take my dinner out of the microwave and put it on the table.

It's roast beef with broccoli, one of my favorites.

I also drink two cups of coffee so I can stay awake.

We're having a history test tomorrow. I need to read the stuff at least three more times.

It might take me all night.

But I'm going to do whatever it takes.

38 TIRED

AFTER MIDNIGHT. My place. I've been studying history for almost three hours.

My head hurts.

I'm tired.

The letters on the page are blurry.

I get up to make another cup of coffee.

But there's only enough to make half a cup.

I get on my crutches, go out the door, and walk to the house to get more coffee.

It's still raining.

The sidewalk is slippery.

I reach the back porch and turn
the doorknob.

My right crutch slips sideways.

I hit the ground.

Pain shoots through my foot.

I get back on my crutches, turn
the doorknob, and go inside.

My foot stops hurting.

But I'm tired of this.

39 HOW PATIENT?

THURSDAY MORNING. My place.

I pour a bowl of cereal and sit at the table.

I'm tired of school.

I'm tired of walking on crutches.

And I'm going to bomb my test in history.

When Harold talked to me in the skills center, he said I would have to keep working and be patient.

How patient do I have to be?

40 ALL OF THEM

HISTORY 101. We're having our essay test today. I know I'm going to bomb.

Dr. Yates comes to the front of the classroom. He has a bald head and wears a suit.

"I'm looking for two things," he says. "First, I'm looking for your mastery of the subject, that you understand the concepts. Second, I'm looking for your ability to express ideas. That means correct grammar and spelling. I also expect you to write neatly."

I know the subject. But I don't have a chance because I can't spell.

The test is about the American Revolution. I read the first question and begin writing.

Clark Daley
Historie 101

When people look at the Decloration of Indpendance, a lot of times they forget aboat the people who singed it and how dangerus it was.

They were all faceing daeath if the Britsh caugt them.

If it wasnt for them, we wuold not have a countrie now.

All of them who singed it were heros.

41 GOING TO DO

AFTERNOON. I get on the bus to go home.

I look out the window and try not to think about the history test.

But the harder I try, the more I think about it.

My foot is destroyed.

My warehouse days are over.

I'm bombing at Jasper College.

What am I going to do?

42 FEEL LIKE

LATER. Home. I walk up the driveway on my crutches.

I hear the clang of weights.

Dad is doing bench presses when I pass the garage.

"Clark, what's up?" he asks.

I step inside. "We had a test in history today. I'm pretty sure I bombed it."

Dad sits up on the weight bench. "What happened?" he asks.

"I studied hard and read everything five times. I knew it

frontwards and backwards. But I know
it wasn't good enough."

"Why do you say that?" he asks.

"Dr. Yates makes a big deal out
of spelling. And my spelling is
terrible."

I see it in Dad's eyes. He knows
how I feel.

"There's something you need to
know," he says. "I've never talked
about it before. When it comes to
reading and spelling, it's always
been hard for me. I almost didn't
graduate from high school."

It's something I've always
wondered about. But I never knew how
to ask him.

"It's hard for you now," Dad
says. "But don't forget what you've
done. You got into college. You're
doing extra to bring up your skills.

And you're not letting your bad foot
stop you."

"That may be true," I say. "But
sometimes it's just too much."

"You also need to know this," Dad
says. "You're doing twenty times
better than you think you are."

He stands and hugs me with all
his strength.

I feel like trying again.

43 YESTERDAY

EVENING. My place. I sit at the table, turn on my laptop, and get on the *Conroy Courier*.

It's hard, but I read all the stories on the front page.

Next, I open my book, *A Wanted Man*.

I finish reading twelve pages. Yesterday I did eight.

44 SEE HIM

MONDAY MORNING. History 101. I walk inside and take my seat. Dr. Yates comes to the front.

"I finished grading your essays last night," he says. "I'm going to read three of them to you now. They are clear, concise, and complete. They also show original thinking."

He begins reading. The first words sound like my paper.

He keeps reading.

It is my paper.

I look down and hope my face

isn't turning red. I've never
thought anything like this would
ever happen to me.

He reads two more papers. But all
I can think about is that he read
mine.

"Try to learn from the essays you
just heard," Dr. Yates says. "When
you get your papers back, you will
have two grades. The first one is
for spelling and grammar. The second
is for the quality of your ideas."

He hands back the papers.

But when I get mine, it doesn't
have any grades.

It just has a note for me to see
him in his office.

45 VERY FAR

LATER. I sit across from Dr. Yates in his office. His shelves are packed with books. I don't see how anyone could ever read so much.

"Clark, I was impressed with the content of your paper and the ideas you discussed," Dr. Yates says. "How much time do you spend studying for this class?"

"Two hours for every one hour of class time. I also do the same for my other classes."

"It shows," he says. "What other

classes are you taking?"

"English 101, Math 101, and Intro to Business."

"What are your goals?" he asks.

"I used to work in a warehouse. But I can't do that kind of work anymore because I hurt my foot. I want to go into business management."

"That's a good goal," Dr. Yates says. "Your efforts are paying off. I've been a professor for a long time. You are going to go very far."

46 MAKING IT

THREE WEEKS LATER. Thursday
afternoon.

I walk up the driveway with my
new cane.

Dr. Beckett said I could use it.
My foot has gotten a lot better.

I look in the backyard.

Dad cooks hamburgers on the
barbecue.

"Clark, it's good to see you
smiling," he says. "How did it go
today?"

I think about all the work I've

done.

I think about the times I've felt
like giving up.

I think about my grades. I got
three C's and a B on my midterms.

I didn't think I would.

But I'm making it.

47 MOVING FORWARD

FRIDAY AFTERNOON. Food Giant Market.
Mom asked me to pick up a few things
for dinner tonight.

I put my cane in a shopping cart
and wheel it down the chips row.

There she is, Ms. Gulliver.
"Clark, how are you doing?" she
asks.

"Everything is fine. I'm working
hard at Jasper."

"What happened to your foot?" she
asks.

"I hurt it in an accident. But

it's doing better now."

"Have you thought any more about
coming back to Edison for College
Day?" she asks.

"What do I have to do?"

"It's next week on Thursday," she
says. "Go to the main office, check
in, and come to my classroom."

"What should I talk about?"

"Tell the students about your
classes at Jasper," she says. "Maybe
you can give them some tips on how
to be successful."

I remember how I lied about
Jasper when I saw her last time.

I felt terrible then.

But I feel good now.

I'm moving forward.

48 STANDING FOR ME

THURSDAY MORNING. Edison High School. I walk on my cane to Ms. Gulliver's class and knock on the door.

Nothing happens.

I get ready to leave.

But she opens the door and gives me that smile.

"Clark, I'm so glad to see you," she says. "I think you're going to help a lot of kids today."

She motions for me to stand at the front of the classroom.

I look at the students and think about myself when I was in their shoes.

"We have a special guest today," Ms. Gulliver says. "It's a pleasure to introduce Mr. Clark Daley. He graduated from here two years ago and is now a student at Jasper Community College. He has some important things to say about how you can be successful after you graduate from here."

It surprises me when she calls me Mr. Daley. But I guess I'm older now.

"I ran into Ms. Gulliver at Food Giant in November," I say. "And I want you to know that I lied to her."

They all sit up. Ms. Gulliver looks surprised.

"I told her I was going to Jasper Community College. But it wasn't true. I was working at a warehouse for Price Mart. I was making good money, and I liked it there. But a forklift ran over my foot and crushed seven bones."

I lift my foot and show them the splint. I remember the pain I felt that day.

"The doctor said I had to get a job where I would not have to be on my feet. That's when I enrolled at Jasper Community College. It's been very hard. But I'm not going to give up."

A kid in the back sits up higher. He looks me in the eye. I wonder if school is hard for him.

Ms. Gulliver smiles. I feel good about what I'm saying.

"School had always been a place of failure for me," I say. "But I got help and I'm working hard. I'm on my way to getting an Associate of Arts degree with a concentration in business administration."

I think about how I felt when I was a ninth grader. I hope I'm saying the right things.

"I know what it's like to turn in your work and know that it's not good enough. I know how it feels when the teacher hands back papers and you don't want anybody to see your grade. I know how it feels to be called upon when you don't know the answer. But it doesn't have to be that way. If you are having trouble, ask for help. You'll be surprised at what happens."

I look at the kid in the back.

He's really listening.

"Ms. Gulliver told us over and over that we could achieve our dreams. I didn't believe her then. But I do believe her now. If you can dream it, you can achieve it."

They all start clapping.

Some of them stand.

Then all of them stand.

They are standing for me.

ACKNOWLEDGMENTS

I would like to express my sincere gratitude to everyone who gave me feedback while I was writing this book.

COFFEE HOUSE WRITERS GROUP: Cori Amoroso, Noemi Arellano-Summer, Jonathan Bay, Breeze Bracken, Jamie Bullen, Nicholas Chiazza, Dan Cragan, Nick Cruz, Paul Dandrea, David Fulps, Julie Hansen, Lynne Horne, Steve Hovland, Peter Ingersoll, Kelly Jeane, Paul Kim, Darian Lane, Peggy Miley, Patti Mobile, Sam Sarkar, John Steiner, Cay Templeton, Anita Thinkofall, Stephen Van Fossen, Sottolin Weng, and Ron Wolff.

GREATER LONG BEACH WRITERS: Leif Beiley, Veronica Cherine, Mary Frances Hill, Donna Nakasone, and Moss Sherian.

SOCIETY OF CHILDREN'S BOOK WRITERS AND ILLUSTRATORS: Jude Atwood, Christine Henderson, Erin Lagerberg, Debbie Menesses, Jenny Parsons, Shiva Sadeghi, Ava Slocum, Desi St. Amat, and Charlotte Van Ryswyck.

Thank you, Pam Sheppard, for your advice on creating this series.

Thank you, Laura Perkins, for your feedback and careful editing.

Thank you, Betty Jean, for your patience, your wisdom, and for being my wife.

ABOUT THE AUTHOR

My dream of becoming a writer started at Whitworth College. I was lucky to have a teacher, Dr. Tammy Reid, who believed in me and encouraged me. After college, I began a career as an educator, teaching reading and English at a middle school in Los Angeles. I went to college at night to earn a doctorate in education. I then served as a high-school principal and district administrator. One of the most important things I have learned is that everyone can achieve success. Set your sights high and work hard every day. If you can dream it, you can achieve it.

FINDING FORWARD BOOKS

At Finding Forward Books, we publish short novels for teens about issues faced by teens. Our goal is to help students improve their reading skills, increase their success in school, and develop positive attitudes.

The books are suitable for all students, including English Learners and those with learning disabilities. Lexile measures range from 390 to 560.

They have been praised in Kirkus Reviews, Publishers Weekly BookLife Reviews, Foreword Clarion Reviews, and BlueInk Reviews.

ADDITIONAL TITLES

TAKEN AWAY. A teen learns to cope with life after his dad is sent to prison.

NO PLACE TO HIDE. A discouraged teen improves his reading skills.

NEVER WANTED. A neglected teen is placed in a foster home.

ALL ALONE. A teen learns to deal with his mom's alcoholism.

KNOCKED DOWN. A football player learns the importance of honesty.

OVERSPRAY. A teen experiences grief after his father dies.

TORN. A student with everything
helps a student who has nothing.

BLUE WALL. A troubled teen battles
back from depression.

LETTERZ. A dyslexic teen learns how
to succeed in school.

CANS. A teen who dreams of attending
college struggles against poverty.

FINDING HOME. A homeless teen gets
the help he needs to succeed.

BRADY'S WAY. A teen who follows
others learns to think for himself.

Finding Forward Books

Short Novels for Teens About

Issues Faced by Teens

www.findingforwardbooks.com